STRESS RE[
CUTE BABY ANIMALS
COLORING BOOK

THIS BOOK BELONGS TO

CUTE BABY ANIMALS COLORING PAGE

Create a color palette and use it to color the pictures

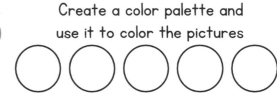

Larva
(ant)

Chick
(chicken)

Fawn
(deer)

Fry
(seahorse)

Lamb
(sheep)

Cygnet
(swan)

Calf
(giraffe)

Hatchling
(turtle)

Calf
(elephant)

Shoat
(domestic pig)

Eaglet
(eagle)

Eyas
(falcon)

Calf
(cow)

Piglet
(pig)

Cub
(leopard)

Puppy
(dog)

Kitten
(raccoon)

Kid
(goat)

Fry
(fish)

Larva
(butterfly)

Tadpole
(frog)

Foal
(horse)

Cub
(lion)

Cub
(bear)

Kit
(Ferret)

Kit
(rabbit)

Duckling
(duck)

Poult
(turkey)

Kit
(fox)

Pup
(prairie dog)

Poult
(pheasant)

Squab
(pigeon)

Foal
(donkey)

Gosling
(goose)

Kitten
(cat)

Pup
(seal)

Owlet
(owl)

ENJOYED COLORING YOUR WAY TO
RELAXATION WITH OUR STRESS RELIEF CUTE
BABY ANIMALS COLORING BOOK?

WE'D LOVE TO HEAR YOUR THOUGHTS! YOUR
FEEDBACK HELPS US CREATE EVEN BETTER
EXPERIENCES.

AFTER YOU'VE FINISHED COLORING, TAKE A
MOMENT TO LEAVE A REVIEW AND SHARE
HOW THESE ADORABLE BABY ANIMALS
HELPED YOU UNWIND. YOUR REVIEW MEANS
THE WORLD TO US AND TO OTHERS LOOKING
FOR THE PERFECT STRESS-RELIEF
COMPANION.

THANK YOU FOR COLORING WITH US!"

WARM REGARDS,
ANNA MARIE RODRIGUES

Made in United States
Troutdale, OR
11/24/2024

25257758R00046